11 P

HILARY SHARPE

Adelaide's
Naughty Granny

Illustrated by Toni Goffe

Methuen Children's Books

To Nicholas and Justin,
Simon, Timothy and Georgina,
Samuel and Mathew,
With love.

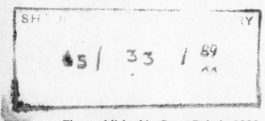
First published in Great Britain 1989
by Methuen Children's Books
A Division of The Octopus Group
Michelin House, 81 Fulham Road, London SW3 6RB

Text copyright © 1989 Hilary Sharpe
Illustrations copyright © 1989 Toni Goffe

Printed in Great Britain by
St. Edmundsbury Press, Bury St Edmunds

British Library Cataloguing in Publication Data

Sharpe, Hilary
    Adelaide's naughty granny.
    I. Title   II. Goffe, Toni   III. Series
    823'.914 [J]

    ISBN 0–416–12762–2

Contents

1

Party Dresses

Adelaide had a naughty granny. Naughty Granny lived in a pretty house in the country with Aunty Vin. Adelaide lived in a big city with Mum and Dad, who kept a sweet shop.

In the school holidays Adelaide often went to stay with Granny and Aunty Vin. She loved going to stay with them because Granny was always doing naughty things!

Sometimes, Aunty Vin would say, 'It's a pity you can't spank a naughty granny!' and then she would sigh and make a sour face.

So that was why Adelaide and Granny called her 'Aunty Vinegar'. But it was a secret name, so as not to hurt her feelings!

And Granny would just smile, and her eyes would twinkle – because *nobody* can spank a naughty granny!

One day, when Adelaide was staying with Naughty Granny and Aunty Vinegar, she had a card from her friend Lucy. It was an invitation to Lucy's sixth birthday party. Lucy lived in a cottage near the village green, just down the lane from Granny's house, and she and Adelaide often played together.

7

'Now Lucy will be nearly as old as me – '
Adelaide laughed, ' – but Granny, I haven't
got my party dress with me.'

'Never mind,' said Granny, 'I will make
you one.'

'Oooh goody,' said Adelaide.

After lunch, Granny got the car out.
There was never much room in Granny's
little car because it was always full of useful
things, like games and maps and books,
interesting pieces of wood, and stones!
Adelaide's dad said he couldn't imagine
how Granny (who was a roly-poly), and
Aunty Vin (who was tall and thin), man
aged

8

to get in at all! But Adelaide loved going out in it. There was always something to do and something to see. When she went out in Dad's car in the big city there was nothing to see but tall buildings.

They all squeezed into the car and set off for town — down the lane, over the river bridge and through the village. As they went up the hill on the other side they had to stop for some sheep who were standing in the middle of the road.

'Tiresome things!' said Aunty Vinegar. Granny honked the horn at them. Soon they were chugging down another hill and into the town square where Granny parked the car.

First, they bought a dress pattern, then Adelaide chose some pretty red material for her dress. While they were getting those, Aunty Vinegar went to buy some cat food for her little black kitten, Sam.

'That shop was having a sale,' she said, 'so I have bought a plastic tablecloth for the kitchen table, then I can wipe it clean when you spill things, Adelaide.'

'What a good idea,' said Granny. And they all went to choose a birthday present for Lucy. Aunty Vinegar suggested a pencil box and Granny suggested a box of magic tricks, but Adelaide couldn't decide.

'I know,' she said, 'I'll get her one of

9

those.' And she pointed to a little china
kitten. It was a black china kitten with a
wavy tail and big blue eyes, just like Sam.

When they got home, Aunty Vinegar
spread the new tablecloth on the kitchen
table. It had pictures of cups and saucers
and plates on it in nice bright colours.

After tea, Granny spread Adelaide's
dress material out on the kitchen table and
laid the pieces of pattern on it.

'Oh-oh,' she said, 'I quite forgot to buy

any sewing thread. You had better get my sewing basket Adelaide, and see if there is any thread the right colour.'

Adelaide fetched the sewing basket. 'Put it on the floor, Adelaide,' said Granny, 'there isn't room on the table.'

She took the box of pins out of the sewing basket and pinned the pattern to the material while Adelaide rummaged through the basket.

'Here we are, Granny,' she said, holding up a reel of red thread, 'will this one match?'

'That's just right,' said Granny, 'what a good job.'

Just then Sam Kitten came running in. He thought Aunty Vinegar might be getting his tea ready.

'Don't leave that sewing basket —' Aunty Vinegar began, but — too late! As soon as Sam saw it he felt sure it was something interesting, and he jumped straight into it! Over went the basket and all the cotton reels and bits and bobs went rolling all over the floor. Sam had a lovely time chasing them!

'There now,' said Aunty Vinegar with a sigh, 'it's a pity you didn't make room for it on the table.' It took them a long time to find everything and tidy up the basket. Sam had his tea and curled up for a sleep.

11

Granny began to cut out the dress. 'These scissors must need sharpening,' she said. 'It is very hard to cut with them.'

When she had finished cutting out the party dress she held up one of the pieces and – 'Goodness me!' she said, 'I have pinned the pattern to the dress material *and* the tablecloth!'

'No wonder it was hard to cut,' said Aunty Vinegar sourly. 'You've cut the tablecloth as well!'

'I am a naughty granny,' sighed Granny. 'I shall have to buy another tablecloth next time we go into town.'

Granny put away the pieces of cut up tablecloth in a drawer, because it was a pity

to waste them, and they might come in useful for something. She sewed up the pretty red material and when she had finished Adelaide had a lovely new party dress to wear for Lucy's party.

On the day before the party, Adelaide wrapped up the little black china Sam in coloured paper, all ready to give to Lucy.

Aunty Vinegar looked at the party invitation card which Granny had left on the mantelpiece.

'Why — it says on the back of this card — "Please come in Fancy Dress"!' she said.

'Oh-oh,' said Granny. 'I didn't notice that.'

'Then I can't wear my pretty new party dress,' said Adelaide, 'and I haven't got a fancy dress to go in.' She looked very disappointed.

'I know,' said Granny. 'You can wear the tablecloth! It has pictures of cups and saucers and plates on it. I will sew it up and you can go as "Tea Time".'

'And I'll wear the tea cosy on my head,' laughed Adelaide.

So Granny sewed up the tablecloth and when she had finished Adelaide had a lovely new tea time party dress.

Granny put two pockets in the tea time dress. In one pocket she put the tea pot from Adelaide's doll's tea set and in the

13

other one she put a plastic knife, fork and spoon, wrapped up in a table napkin.

When the party was over, Adelaide said, 'Lucy loved the little black china Sam – and Granny! I won a prize for my "Tea Time" fancy dress!'

'Well, I'm glad that tablecloth wasn't wasted,' said Aunty Vinegar.

'And when we have a party here you can wear your pretty red party dress, Adelaide, and that won't be wasted either!' said Granny, and she chuckled, because you can't spank a naughty granny!

14

2

Wet Wellies

The next time Adelaide went to stay with Naughty Granny and Aunty Vinegar, the weather was cold and wet. Adelaide had to play indoors, but as soon as the sun came out, Granny said, 'Let's go for a walk along the riverbank and feed the ducks.'

'You'd better put your macs and wellies on then,' said Aunty Vinegar. 'It's going to rain again.'

So they put their macs and wellies on and Granny put some bread in her pocket for the ducks.

'Don't get your feet wet, Adelaide,' said Aunty Vinegar, 'I don't want you catching cold.'

'No, Aunty Vin,' said Adelaide. Off they went, down the lane to the river. Sure enough, as soon as they got to the river bank, it began to rain quite hard.

'Never mind,' said Granny. 'We'll shelter under these bushes and sing songs until it stops.'

They crawled under some rho-dodendron bushes and sat on the twisty

15

branches. They sang 'Incy Wincy Spider' and 'Rain, Rain, Go Away'. A blackbird came and sang with them.

When the rain stopped there were lots of lovely puddles. Granny said, 'Let's jump in them and see who can splash the highest.'

Granny won, and Adelaide said, 'I think I've got some rain inside my wellies.'

She took her wellies off. 'Yak,' she said. 'Wet socks.'

'Never mind,' said Granny. 'Take them off and we'll hang them on the bushes to dry. The blackbird will look after them for you.'

They walked along the river bank and presently they saw the ducks. Granny put her hand into her pocket to get the bread, but – 'Ugggh,' said Granny, 'the rain has got in first and made the bread all squidgey. It's stuck to my pocket.'

'Oh, Granny,' said Adelaide, 'Aunty Vinegar won't be very pleased!'

'But the ducks won't mind,' said Granny, scooping out bits of squidgey bread. 'We will have a duck feeding competition.'

She gave some of the bread to Adelaide and they took turns to throw it into the river. When the brown duck got it, Adelaide won, and when the white duck got it, Granny won. Granny won twice and Adelaide won three times!

16

Then a piece of Granny's bread landed on the bank. Both the ducks looked for it, but they couldn't find it, so Granny pushed it into the water. Both ducks dived for it. Granny leaned over to watch.

'Which one has got it Granny?' cried Adelaide, jumping up and down with excitement.

'I can't quite see,' Granny said, leaning further over the bank. And then – Granny's foot slipped on the muddy bank and one of her wellies went splash! – into the

river! Adelaide clapped her hands to her mouth!

'Oh-oh,' said Granny, 'now Aunty Vinegar *will* have something to be cross about!'

The wellie floated along on the water like a boat. The ducks took no notice of it at all. Soon, it stuck in the mud at the edge of the bank. Granny reached out for it and Adelaide held her breath in case Granny fell in. Then, just as Granny was going to pull it out it filled up with water and sank out of reach.

'Your poor wellie,' cried Adelaide, 'it will be so cold in the river.'

'The ducks will take care of it for me,' said Granny. 'And tomorrow we'll bring a garden rake and fish it out. Now, shall we have a hopping race?'

They set off, hop, hop, hop, and Granny was soon going puff, puff, puff. When they reached the rhododendron bushes the blackbird was still singing, and there were Adelaide's socks, looking like bright red flowers in the sunshine.

'I nearly forgot my socks, Granny,' Adelaide said. She sat down and put her socks on again. Granny sat down and got her breath back.

'My socks are quite dry,' Adelaide said.

'That's because the blackbird looked after them for you,' said Granny.

18

When they got home Aunty Vinegar said, 'It rained so hard I got quite worried about you.'

'We sheltered in some bushes,' said Granny. 'Adelaide's feet are quite dry, but I lost a wellie in the river and the bread has made a squidgey mess in my pocket.'

'It's a pity you can't spank a naughty granny,' Aunty Vinegar sighed, when

19

Granny had told her all about the bread
and the ducks and how she lost her wellie.
'AND – we're going to have fish fingers
and chips for tea!'

'Oooh goody,' said Adelaide. 'Can
Naughty Granny have some as well?'

'Yes, I suppose so,' said Aunty Vinegar,
and then she smiled a little smile and said,
'I wonder if the brown duck or the white
duck got the last piece of squidgey bread?'

Adelaide laughed, and Granny's eyes
twinkled as she shook the vinegar bottle
over her fish fingers and chips because you
can't spank a naughty granny!

3

Grand Spring Fair

Once, when Adelaide was staying with Naughty Granny and Aunty Vinegar during the Easter holidays, there was a Grand Spring Fair in the Village Hall. Everyone in the village was helping. Adelaide had brought some of her toys from home for the toy stall.

'I have baked some cakes for the cake stall and Aunty Vin is giving some of her spring vegetables and plants from the garden,' said Granny.

The evening before the fair, Mr Mimby the grocery man called.

'Herey'are, me dear,' he said to Granny. 'I've brought you some nice clean cardboard boxes to put your cakes in.'

'I should like some of those for my vegetables and plants,' said Aunty Vinegar.

'I'll come and help you collect them, me dear,' said Mr Mimby.

So they all went out into the garden. While they were out, Sam Kitten decided to play hide and seek in one of the boxes. Granny came back with an armful of spring vegetables. She popped them in the neares box – and out popped Sam, just like a jack-in-the-box!

'Goodness, whatever was that?' gasped Granny. She stepped back and bumped into Aunty Vinegar, who dropped the cabbages she was carrying. They rolled across the kitchen floor and tripped up Mr Mimby who had just come in with a box of plants.

'Whooops!' he said, and dropped the box on to the floor.

'Oh, poor Sam!' cried Adelaide. 'You

nearly squashed him, Granny.'

'And just look at my poor plants,' said Aunty Vinegar sourly. 'There is soil from them all over the kitchen floor.'

Luckily the plants weren't damaged and Mr Mimby helped Aunty Vinegar to pack them into the boxes again.

'Oh-oh,' said Granny. 'I'm afraid I'll have to wash the kitchen floor.'

'I'll help you, Granny,' said Adelaide.

Next day they took Granny's useful things out of the car to make room for all the boxes and drove down to the village. There were so many cars that they had to park beside the church, across the green. Mr Mimby saw them from his shop and came across to help carry everything to the hall. Everyone was busy getting ready. There were trestle tables all round the room, and stalls outside on the grass.

When they had taken the cakes and vegetables and toys to the stalls that were going to sell them, they all went to help sort out the jumble that was on a big table on the grass outside. As soon as the church clock struck two the hall was full of people buying things.

Granny spotted some nice bright stripey jumpers among the jumble.

'I think I shall buy one of those,' she said to Aunty Vinegar, who was in charge of the

23

stall. 'They would be just right for garden-ing in the winter.'

'You had better try one on then, before they are all sold,' said Aunty Vinegar.

Granny took off her coat and tried several of the jumpers. When she had chosen one she said, 'Where did I put my coat, Adelaide? I can't see it anywhere.'

'Goodness, Granny, I hope it hasn't been sold with the jumble,' Adelaide said.

'So do I,' said Granny. 'It's my best one.'

'There it is!' exclaimed Aunty Vinegar. 'That lady is just trying it on.' She ran up to the lady and explained that the coat wasn't for sale.

'You had better put it on again,' Aunty Vinegar said, looking all flustered. 'The lady wasn't at all pleased when I took it off her.'

Adelaide took Granny off to look at the other stalls. At the toy stall they saw Adelaide's friend Lucy.

'I have bought a nice jigsaw,' said Lucy.

'I think I will buy one, too,' said Adelaide.

They all had a go at the hoop-la stall.

'I would like to win that little dolly-in-a-cot,' said Adelaide.

'Me too!' said Lucy. They all tried to win it, but they missed. Granny won a bottle of tomato sauce!

'Never mind,' said Granny. 'I see your mummy is selling raffle tickets Lucy. I'll buy some for all of us.'

When they got back to the jumble stall Mr Mimby had come to help as well. 'I think we will go and fetch some tea, Adelaide,' said Granny.

The tea ladies were very busy, so Granny got a tray and poured out five cups of tea. Then she noticed that the sugar bowl was empty. She saw a big jar of sugar on a shelf and filled the sugar bowl.

'Thank you, me dear,' said Mr Mimby. 'I was just ready for a cuppa.' Lucy handed him the sugar bowl and he put three large spoonfuls of sugar in his tea and took a big gulp.

'Aaaah – grumpphh – phooo – !' he spluttered. 'It's *horrible!*'

Aunty Vinegar had put one small spoonful in her tea, but when she sipped it she pulled a very sour face.

'Ugh – oof! Someone has put salt in this tea instead of sugar!' she gasped.

'Oh, Granny, you are naughty,' Adelaide giggled. 'You must have filled the sugar bowl with salt!'

'I'm glad I don't take sugar,' said Lucy.

Granny decided she had better go very quickly and get some fresh cups!

By the end of the afternoon nearly everything had been sold. All Aunty Vinegar's nice fresh vegetables and plants had gone, but there was still quite a lot of jumble left. Aunty Vinegar treated herself to a pair of wellies for gardening, and Granny treated her to a bobble hat. She was just going to buy a cake from the cake stall when Lucy's mummy began calling out the winners numbers of the raffle tickets. Granny and Adelaide didn't win anything, but Aunty Vinegar won – a little dolly-in-a-cot!

'Goodness,' said Adelaide, 'it is just like the one on the hoop-la stall.'

'It *is* the one on the hoop-la stall, me dear,' said Mr Mimby. 'I won it, but I haven't got any little girls to give it to, so I gave it to the raffle as an extra prize.'

'I think I know a little girl who might like it, if she's good,' said Aunty Vinegar.

'Oh thank you, Aunty Vin,' said Adelaide. 'I will play with it when I go to Lucy's house.'

When they were ready to go home, Granny said, 'Oh-oh, I quite forgot to buy that cake.'

'It's too late now,' said Aunty Vinegar. 'They've sold out.'

'Naughty Granny,' Adelaide sighed.

But Granny just smiled a little smile, because you can't spank a naughty granny!

4

Sand and Swingboats

One day in the summer holidays, Granny and Aunty Vinegar decided they would all have a day at the seaside. They took Lucy with them as well, but before they could start they had to take most of Granny's useful things out of the car to make room for Lucy and Adelaide and the picnic basket.

It was a lovely hot sunny day and they parked the car on the promenade and went straight down to the beach.

'It will be a nice change to sit in the sun and do nothing,' said Aunty Vinegar.

Adelaide and Lucy made a sandcastle. Granny sat in a deckchair and Aunty Vinegar spread a rug on the sand. Presently Aunty Vinegar said, 'This sun is too hot.' She put up the big beach umbrella and sat in the shade.

Adelaide said, 'Will you help us to find some shells to put on our sandcastle, Granny?'

'Right,' said Granny, 'we will take your seaside bucket to put them in.'

They collected lots of shells, stones and

29

seaweed. When they got back, Aunty Vinegar was fast asleep.

Lucy said, 'I'll make a pattern with the seaweed.' She put it all round the sandcastle and made a little wall of stones. Adelaide dug a moat and stuck a paper flag on top of the sandcastle. Aunty Vinegar still slept!

'Let's cover Aunty's feet with sand,' whispered Naughty Granny.

'Oooh yes,' whispered Adelaide. So they covered Aunty's feet, and then they covered her legs, and then her tummy, and even her arms!

When Aunty Vinegar woke up, she tried to sit up, but she couldn't because of all the sand!

'OH! Whatever is all this sand doing on top of me?' she cried.

'We'll help you up Aunty,' said Adelaide. She and Lucy took one of Aunty Vinegar's hands and Granny took the other.

'Heave ho!' Granny cried. 'Ups-a-daisy!'

Aunty Vinegar sat up so suddenly that Granny nearly overbalanced. She knocked the big beach umbrella over, right on top of poor Aunty Vinegar!

'Pshwa! Ugh! I nearly got a mouthful of sand,' Aunty Vinegar spluttered.

'Never mind. It's time we had our lunch and I've got something much nicer than

sand for you,' said Granny, as she
unpacked the picnic basket.

When they had finished, Lucy saw some
donkeys lower down the beach.

'Please, could we have a donkey ride?'
she asked Granny.

'Yes of course,' said Granny. 'I'll come
with you.'

The donkeys trotted along the beach.
Adelaide was on a donkey called Snowball
and Lucy was on Smokey. Granny bought
some carrots at one of the stalls on the
Promenade to give to the donkeys. When
the ride was over they all walked back to
Aunty Vinegar. Suddenly there was a loud
Hee-Haw! behind them!

31

'Goodness, whatever is that?' cried Granny.

'Oh, Granny, Snowball and Smokey want some more carrot,' laughed Adelaide. 'And they've brought their friends with them! What will Aunty Vinegar say?'

Granny turned round, and there were all the donkeys, waiting for some carrot!

'Hey,' shouted the donkey man, 'bring my donkeys back!'

Granny went quickly back to the donkey man, and all the donkeys followed her. She gave the donkeys the rest of the carrots — but there were a lot of donkeys! Granny had to go and buy some more carrots so that she could give them all a piece.

By this time, a lot of people had stopped to watch, and they all laughed and cheered as Granny fed the donkeys!

When they got back to Aunty Vinegar again she had quite a lot to say! 'Whatever next!' she cried. 'Leading all those donkeys astray! I think we'd better move further down the beach.'

They went further along, where the beach was quieter, and had a bathe in the sea. While they were getting dried and dressed, Adelaide said, 'I can hear some music.'

They all listened and Aunty Vinegar said, 'I think it's a band playing somewhere.'

'I know what it is,' said Granny. 'It's a fair. Look, you can see the lights at the end of the promenade. Would you like to go?'

'Oooh, yes please,' Adelaide and Lucy said together. They went back to the car and drove to the fairground.

Adelaide and Lucy went on a roundabout, then Granny said, 'I like the swingboats, let's go and find them.'

Granny and Adelaide got in the first one and Lucy and Aunty Vinegar got in the second. The man gave them a push to start them off. They pulled hard on the ropes.

It was grand! 'HIGHER!' shouted Adelaide, and 'FASTER!' shouted Lucy, 'let's see who can swing highest!'

When the ride was over Aunty Vinegar said, 'I *did* enjoy that, I haven't been in a swingboat for years!'

Just then, some boys came running past, shouting 'Hee-haw, hee-haw,' and 'Carrots!'

'What cheeky boys,' exclaimed Aunty Vinegar. 'They must have seen Granny feeding those donkeys!'

The boys ran off laughing, but when they looked round for Granny, they couldn't see her anywhere. She had just disappeared. They looked and looked, until suddenly, Adelaide saw her on a roundabout of horses that went up and down, up and down!

'We thought you were lost, Granny,' said Adelaide.

'It's a pity you can't spank naughty grannies who get lost,' sighed Aunty Vinegar. 'Now it's time to go home.'

'Oh-oh,' said Granny, 'I'm sorry – but when I was a little girl I used to *love* the horses that went up and down, up and down.'

'Couldn't we just have a ride on those horses that go up and down, up and down, too?' pleaded Adelaide.

'Oh, please!' said Lucy. 'They're nearly as nice as the donkeys.'

34

'Very well,' said Aunty Vinegar. And they all enjoyed the ride so much that they had another ride on the horses that go up and down, up and down.

As they drove back home along the promenade, they saw the donkeys again, going home one behind the other. The donkey man waved to them.

'Don't let them see you, Granny,' Adelaide said. 'They might want some more carrots!'

But Granny just smiled, because you can't spank a naughty granny!

5
Sam and Two Patches

Once, when Adelaide was staying with Naughty Granny and Aunty Vinegar, Lucy's mummy brought her new puppy round and asked Granny if she would look after him for the day, as she had to go out.

'He's called Patch, because he has a black patch on his ear,' Granny said, giving him to Adelaide to hold.

'Oh Granny, he's lovely,' said Adelaide. 'But what will Sam Kitten say?'

'I hope they won't fight,' said Aunty Vinegar.

'We'll make sure they don't meet,' said Granny.

Adelaide and Granny took Patch for a walk to the village green. When they got back Patch was tired, so Granny took him into the dining room to have a sleep.

'He'll be all right in there,' she said.

By and by, Aunty Vinegar said, 'What's that funny noise?'

They all listened, and – 'Squeeeak – thump – wow-oww' went the funny noise.

'It isn't Sam,' said Granny, 'he's in the kitchen.'

'I think Patch has woken up,' Adelaide said. They went into the dining room – and there was the tablecloth, rolling about on the floor!

'Goodness,' said Granny. 'Patch has pulled the cloth off the table and got himself all tangled up in it.'

'It's a good job he hasn't torn it,' said Aunty Vinegar when they had unrolled Patch, 'but he's left dirty paw marks on it.'

'Never mind,' said Granny. 'I'll wash it.'

Adelaide took Patch into the garden to play, so Granny shut Sam in the dining room this time. But – oh dear! – she had

37

forgotten about the open window! Sam
jumped out, into the garden — right in
front of Patch! They looked at each other —
then Patch wagged his tail and Sam began
to purr!

'I don't think they know that dogs are
supposed to chase cats,' Adelaide laughed.

So they all played in the garden until tea
time. When Granny called Adelaide in for
tea, Adelaide said, 'Will Patch be all right if
I leave him alone in the garden, Granny?'

'Yes,' said Granny. 'The gate's shut, so he can't get out. And he's got Sam to play with.'

But when it was time to take Patch home – Sam was fast asleep under a tree and there was no sign of Patch!

'Oh, Granny,' said Adelaide, 'he must have got out through the hedge.'

'T'ch, t'ch,' said Aunty Vinegar, 'we should have put him on a lead.'

'We had better go and look for him,' Granny said.

Granny and Adelaide went up the lane to look for him and Aunty Vinegar went

down the lane. Granny and Adelaide had almost reached the end of the lane when Granny said, 'There he is!' And there was Patch, sitting beside a garden gate.

Granny picked him up and carried him home, but when they got there, Aunty Vinegar said, 'I have found Patch!'

'So have I,' gasped Granny. Each of them was holding a puppy with a black patch on one ear. They looked like twins!

'Goodness,' said Granny, 'which one is Patch?'

'I know, Granny,' Adelaide said, pointing to the puppy Aunty Vinegar was holding. 'That one is Patch, I remember his blue collar. You have found the wrong puppy.'

'Oh dear, I am a naughty granny,' said Granny. 'They are so alike they must be brothers. It's a good job this one is wearing a red collar, I had better take him home again quickly.'

Aunty Vinegar sighed, but there was a twinkle in Granny's eye, because you can't spank a naughty granny!

6
Secret Shopping

At the end of the summer holidays, Aunty Vinegar had a birthday, and Granny had planned a surprise party for her.

When she had opened her birthday cards, Aunty Vinegar said, 'I think I'll go to town and treat myself to some new shoes.'

'We can all go together,' said Granny. 'Adelaide and I have some secret shopping to do.'

'Oh – SSSsshhh Granny,' said Adelaide, bouncing up and down with excitement! Aunty Vinegar looked puzzled!

In the village, Granny stopped the car to have a word with Mr Mimby, the grocery man. Mr Mimby had a big smile on his face.

'Happy Birthday, me dear,' he said to Aunty Vinegar.

'Goodness,' said Aunty Vinegar, looking puzzled, 'however did you know?'

When they got to town Aunty Vinegar went off to buy her shoes and Granny and Adelaide went to the biggest shop in town to look for presents for Aunty Vinegar.

'I think she would like one of these nice bright cushions for her chair,' said Granny.

'And I will buy her one of these pretty brooches,' said Adelaide.

'Now,' said Granny, 'I have to get some more wool for Aunty Vinegar's jumper. Do you want to look at the toys while I get it?'

'Yes please,' said Adelaide. She had been saving her pocket money because she wanted to do some secret shopping of her own and had been wondering how to do it without Granny knowing.

'I'll come back here for you in a few minutes,' said Granny. 'Don't go away.'

Next, they came to the cake shop. Granny had ordered a really nice birthday cake for Aunty Vinegar. The cake shop man

packed it carefully so that it wouldn't get
squashed.

When they got to the café where they
were going to have lunch there was no sign
of Aunty Vinegar, so Granny and Adelaide
chose a table. As she sat down, Granny
dropped one of her parcels. It bounced on
the floor and went tinkle, tinkle, tinkle!

'Whatever is that?' Adelaide asked in
astonishment.

'Oh-oh,' said Granny, picking up the
tinkly parcel. 'It was going to be a secret.
It's an un-birthday present for Sam Kitten.
It is a ball with a bell inside so that he won't
lose it.'

'Oh, Granny,' laughed Adelaide, 'I'd better tell you my secret. I've bought him an
un-birthday present as well! Look!'

She opened her secret parcel and showed Granny a little grey clockwork mouse. 'Sam will love that,' said Granny, winding up the mouse. 'Let's see him run across the table.'

She let go of the clockwork mouse and before she could catch him again – he had run across the table and on to the floor!

'Oh – OHH – it's a mouse!' screamed the lady at the next table. While Granny was trying to explain that it was only a clock-work one, Adelaide pounced on it just like Sam and popped it back in Granny's bag.

Just then Aunty Vinegar came into the café. 'I hope I'm not late,' she said. 'I have had a nice morning. I have bought some birthday shoes and a birthday dress!'

'Ooh goody,' said Adelaide. 'You can wear them for your – er, your – '

'SSSSHHHHH!' said Granny sternly. Aunty Vinegar looked very puzzled!

After lunch they went back to the car. Granny opened her bag to get out her car keys – and they weren't there. She couldn't find them anywhere!

'Oh-oh,' said Granny, 'I must have dropped them.'

'Oh dear, you are a naughty granny,' sighed Aunty Vinegar.'And you have got *such* a lot of shopping. I think I had better stay here and look after it while you and Adelaide go and look for the keys.'

'No peeking,' said Granny, putting down her shopping bags, and they hurried off. They tried the big shop and the café – but no keys. Then they went to the cake shop. The cake shop man wasn't very pleased.

'Are these your keys, madam?' he asked. And there were Granny's keys, covered in chocolate cream!

'There,' said Granny, 'they must have fallen out of my bag when I took my purse out.'

'They fell into a chocolate cream cake

and quite spoilt it,' said the cake shop man, wiping the keys on a tissue and handing them to Granny.

'Never mind,' said Granny. 'I'll pay for it. We can put chocolate drops over the spoilt bit.'

'Now we have got *two* birthday cakes!' Adelaide laughed.

'And not much time before the party guests arrive,' puffed Granny as they hurried back to the car.

When they got home again, Granny said to Aunty Vinegar, 'Adelaide and I are going to get the tea ready today, so you can sit in the garden in the sunshine.'

'That will be nice,' said Aunty Vinega.

47

And she put on her birthday dress and her birthday shoes and sat in the garden with her favourite book. Soon, she was fast asleep.

Granny and Adelaide bustled around. Adelaide tied a big stripey ribbon round Sam kitten's neck and Granny put flowers all round the dining room and they set the table with the best china. Granny put on her best dress and Adelaide put on her pretty red party dress.

Then Mr Mimby came with all the party food Granny had ordered. He helped Granny and Adelaide to put it out on the table.

They quickly wrapped the presents and Granny was just sticking the labels on them – when the party guests arrived!

'Pphhewww!' puffed Granny. 'We have just finished in time! Go and tell Aunty Vin that tea is ready, Adelaide.'

What a surprise Aunty Vinegar got when she went into the dining room! All her friends were there, waiting to sing 'Happy Birthday To You!'

She was just cutting her two birthday cakes when there was a knock at the door and Mr Mimby came in.

'Here y'are, me dear,' he said to Aunty Vinegar, 'groceries.'

'Goodness,' said Aunty Vinegar looking

puzzled. 'But – it isn't grocery day today!'

'Special delivery,' said Mr Mimby with a big smile. 'Seeing as it's someone's birthday!'

And instead of groceries, the box was full of birthday presents! Everyone had left their gifts on the kitchen table and Mr Mimby had crept in and put them in his box.

'Well, I never!' gasped Aunty Vinegar.

While Granny cut a big slice of cake for Mr Mimby, Aunty Vinegar opened her presents.

'Why, here is an un-birthday present for Sam Kitten, from Granny and Adelaide,' she said when she had nearly got to the bottom of the box. 'A pretty brooch and a nice bright cushion. How odd!'

Granny and Adelaide looked very puzzled. Then Aunty Vinegar looked rather sour. 'And whatever am I supposed to do with a tinkly ball and a clockwork mouse?' she cried.

'Oh, Granny,' laughed Adelaide, 'you are naughty, you have got the labels mixed up. The cushion and the brooch are for you, Aunty, and the ball and mouse are for Sam!'

'Oh, that is much better,' said Aunty Vinegar, throwing the ball for Sam to chase. 'And there are *more* un-birthday presents. One for Granny from Adelaide and one for Adelaide from Granny! So *that's* what all that secret shopping was all about this morning!'

'Well, I never!' Granny and Adelaide exclaimed together, and Granny's eyes twinkled, because you can't spank a naughty granny, especially on Aunty Vinegar's birthday!

7

Ladies to Tea

One autumn day, when Adelaide was staying with Naughty Granny, Aunty Vinegar looked out of the kitchen window and said, 'My, what a mess. The wind has blown leaves all over the garden! I think you had better go out and clear them up, Adelaide.'

Adelaide went into the garden. Sam Kitten came too. He wasn't much help but he had a wonderful time chasing the leaves.

Presently, Granny came out to help. 'There are some nice leaves here,

Adelaide,' she said, 'we will save the best ones to make a leaf picture.'

'What's a leaf picture, Granny?' Adelaide asked.

'It's a picture made with leaves instead of paint,' Granny said.

When they had finished tidying the garden, they took a bundle of leaves into the kitchen. Adelaide put them on the table while Granny found a big piece of stiff paper, a pot of glue and a brush.

'There are some ladies coming to tea this afternoon,' Aunty Vinegar said, 'so don't make a mess, Adelaide.'

'No, Aunty,' said Adelaide.

Aunty Vinegar went into the dining room to set the table with her best lace tablecloth and the best china. Sam came into the kitchen to see if he was missing anything.

'Now,' said Granny, 'we'll take turns to choose a leaf and stick it on the paper.'

Adelaide chose a big yellow sycamore leaf, put a dab of glue on the back and stuck it in the middle of the paper. Granny chose a brown oak leaf and stuck it in the top corner. Adelaide took a copper beech leaf and put it at the bottom and then Granny found a whole branch of yellowy-green willow leaves and glued them down on one side.

'Granny!' Adelaide laughed, 'you are naughty, that's cheating!'

'Never mind,' said Granny. 'Now you know how to do it, you can finish the picture yourself while I make the sandwiches for tea.'

So Adelaide went on sticking down the leaves until she had covered all the paper.

'There,' said Granny, 'now you have made an autumn leaf picture. That's very pretty.'

She reached across the table to pick up the picture and — knocked the glue pot over! A stream of sticky glue spread across the table and went drip — drip — drip on to the kitchen chair! Sam fled!

'Oh Granny, what will Aunty Vinegar say?' gasped Adelaide.

'Never mind,' said Granny. 'Go and put your picture somewhere safe and then come and help me clear the glue up.'

Adelaide took her precious picture into the dining room. Aunty Vinegar was just going out to the garden to pick some flowers for the table.

'That is very nice, Adelaide,' she said. 'Put it on the sideboard, then the ladies can see it when they come to tea.'

When Adelaide got back to the kitchen, Granny gave her a wet cloth, and they both mopped up the glue on the table and wiped it clean again. Sam poked his head round the door.

'I'd better put Sam out of the way,' Granny said, 'in case there's any glue on the floor. I don't want him to get his paws in it.'

She took him out, and Adelaide was just rinsing out the cloths ready to wipe the glue off the chair, when in came Aunty Vinegar with a bunch of Michaelmas daisies.

'I think I've got a stone in my shoe,' she said – and sat down on the kitchen chair!

'Oh dear!' said Adelaide.

'Ooh – ugh – whatever is this nasty sticky stuff all over the chair?' cried Aunty Vinegar.

54

She stood up quickly, before she could
stick to it!

'There now,' said Granny, coming back
into the kitchen. 'I'm afraid it's my fault, I
spilt some glue. Never mind, it will wash
out.'

'It's a good job I've still got my old clothes
on,' said Aunty Vinegar sourly. 'I'd better
go and change.'

'Take the sandwiches into the dining
room on your way, will you?' Granny said,
as she and Adelaide began to clean the glue
off the chair. When they had finished,

Granny put the Michaelmas daisies into a vase.

'We'll put these on the dining room table and then we'll go and get ready for the ladies,' said Granny.

Granny opened the dining room door and – oh dear! There was Sam on the table, eating the bloater paste sandwiches!

'Oh-oh,' said Granny. 'I quite forgot I'd put Sam in here out of the way!'

Sam looked very guilty. He jumped down off the table – and over went the milk jug!

'Naughty Sam!' Adelaide said. 'Aunty Vinegar's best tablecloth!'

'Well,' said Granny, 'we will just have to use the second best tablecloth – and make some more sandwiches.'

She quickly cleared the table and set it again with the second best tablecloth. Adelaide took the best tablecloth into the kitchen and put it to soak in a bowl of water. Then they both made some more sandwiches. Adelaide put Sam out in the garden this time.

When the ladies arrived for tea they were so delighted with Adelaide's leaf picture that they asked if they could have it.

Aunty Vinegar looked rather puzzled to see the second best tablecloth on the tea table, and even more puzzled to see her best lace one blowing on the clothes line in the garden, but she didn't ask what had happened, she just said, 'T'ch, t'ch,' and shook her head!

Granny didn't say a word, but her eyes twinkled, because you can't spank a naughty granny!

8

Holly and Snow

One snowy day just before Christmas, Adelaide was making Christmas cards with coloured paper shapes when Aunty Vinegar said, 'I can't find the box of Christmas decorations anywhere.'

'H'm,' said Granny, 'I wonder where I put it? Never mind, we can make some more.'

'Can we pick some holly too?' Adelaide asked.

'If it's stopped snowing,' said Aunty

Vinegar. It had, so they all went out. Aunty Vinegar said she had some shopping to do in the village.

Granny took Aunty Vinegar's pocket knife to cut the holly with and Adelaide took some string to tie up the bunches. Aunty Vinegar took her shopping basket and set off down the lane to the village.

As they walked across the field to the holly bushes, Adelaide said, 'Look, we have made wellie tracks.'

They looked back, and there was a wobbly line of little wellie tracks and a wobbly line of big wellie tracks.

'Let's make a wellie track pattern,' said Granny. 'You take little steps and I'll take big steps.'

So they walked with big and little steps and then they ran with big and little steps. By and by Granny called out, 'All change!' and Adelaide took big steps and Granny took little steps. Then, by mistake, Granny bumped into Adelaide and they both fell down in the snow.

'Oh Granny, you are naughty,' Adelaide giggled, as they brushed the snow off each other. 'You have spoilt the wellie track pattern.'

'Never mind,' said Granny. 'Look at the trees, don't they look pretty all covered with snow?'

She reached up and shook one of the trees. The snow fell down with a plop.

'Oooh, it's cold,' said Adelaide, as some of the snow fell on her. She shook one of the trees and Granny jumped quickly out of the way.

'Missed me,' Granny chuckled. Then they ran from tree to tree, trying to catch each other under the falling snow. Presently, Granny shook a big tree at the edge of the field. Some of the branches overhung the road. The snow fell off with a *plop* – and – 'OH – Ugh!' said a rather cross voice from the other side of the hedge.

'Oh-oh,' said Granny, 'that sounded like Aunty Vinegar's voice, I think we'd better run!'

They ran across the field to the holly bushes. 'Look,' cried Adelaide. 'There are some lovely red berries on these bushes.'

Granny put her hand in her pocket to get Aunty Vinegar's knife – and it wasn't there!

'Granny! What will Aunty Vinegar say?' said Adelaide. 'We had better go and find it.'

They went back and looked in all the places where they had shaken the snow off the trees, but they couldn't find Aunty Vinegar's knife anywhere.

'I must have dropped it when I sat down in the snow,' said Granny. So back they went to the wellie track pattern and looked in the place where Granny had fallen.

'Here it is, Naughty Granny!' Adelaide exclaimed suddenly, holding up Aunty Vinegar's knife.

'Oh goody,' said Granny. 'Now we had

better be quick or we will be late for dinner.'

Back they went again to the holly bushes and soon they had two big bunches tied up with Adelaide's string.

When they got home again Granny said, 'We will leave the holly outside until after dinner.' So they put it down carefully near the back door and went into the kitchen.

'There are some scraps for the birds here, Adelaide,' Aunty Vinegar said. 'Will you put them out before you have your dinner.'

'Yes, Aunty,' said Adelaide. So while Aunty Vinegar dished up the dinner, Adelaide took some pieces of bread, some

nuts and suet, and some bacon rind and scattered them outside the back door. Soon there were sparrows and chaffinches darting in amongst the bigger birds, and several cheeky robins, all having a noisy feast.

'My, they were hungry,' Adelaide laughed.

While they had their dinner, Granny and Adelaide told Aunty Vinegar about the wellie pattern they had made in the snow.

'I hope you didn't get cold falling about in the snow,' Aunty Vinegar said. 'When I went to the village some snow fell off a tree, right on top of me!'

Adelaide looked sideways at Granny, and Granny said, 'Oh, dear, I hope it didn't hurt you?'

'Luckily it didn't,' said Aunty Vinegar, 'but it made my hat all wet.'

When they had washed up the dinner things Aunty Vinegar brought in the holly. But she didn't look very pleased.

'Couldn't you find any holly with berries on it?' she asked. She held up the bunches of holly and – there wasn't one berry to be seen!

'Goodness!' said Granny. 'Those greedy birds must have eaten all the scraps and then had our holly berries for pudding.'

'It's a pity you didn't bring the holly

inside,' said Aunty Vinegar.

'We'll make some plasticine berries instead,' said Granny. She got a stick of bright red plasticine and cut it into little squares. Then she and Adelaide rolled them round and round until they were just the same size as holly berries. When they had put the holly up they stuck the red plasticine berries in amongst the leaves.

'There,' said Granny. 'No one except the birds will know they aren't real berries.'

Presently they all sat down at the table to make paper chains and soon they had a big pile of gaily coloured decorations. Granny cut some stars out of silver paper to hang amongst them.

Aunty Vinegar fetched the steps, and while she and Granny hung up the paper chains, Adelaide finished making her Christmas cards. She made specially nice ones for Granny and Aunty Vinegar.

Granny finished hanging the last of the paper chains and looked round the room.

'There,' she said. 'Doesn't it look nice and festive! OH! Now I can see the box with the Christmas decorations in it – I put it on top of the bookcase!'

'Well,' said Aunty Vinegar with a sigh, 'I suppose we can use them next year.'

And Granny's eyes twinkled, because you can't spank a naughty granny!